D0435137

T1-BKC-646

SENTINEL

Story: Sean McKeever

Art by UDON

Pencils and Inks: Vriens, Heilig, Hepburn, and Vedder

Colors: Hou, Yan, and Yeung   UDON Chief: Erik Ko   Letters: Cory Petit

Assistant Editor: Andy Schmidt   Editor: Marc Sumerak   Editor in Chief: Joe Quesada

President: Bill Jemas

REBUILDING

PART 4

MARVEL   Spotlight

VISIT US AT
www.abdopublishing.com

Reinforced library bound edition published in 2007 by Spotlight, a division of the ABDO Publishing Group, Edina, Minnesota. Spotlight produces high-quality reinforced library bound editions for schools and libraries. Published by agreement with Marvel Characters, Inc.

Library of Congress Cataloging-in-Publication Data

McKeever, Sean.
Sentinel / [story, Sean McKeever ; pencils and inks, UDON ... et al.].
v. cm.
Cover title.
Revisions of issues 1-6 of the serial Sentinel.
"Marvel Age."
Contents: #1. Salvage -- #2. Discovery -- #3. Pet project -- #4. Rebuilding -- #5. Test mission -- #6. Primary targets.
ISBN-13: 978-1-59961-316-1 (v. 1)
ISBN-10: 1-59961-316-6 (v. 1)
ISBN-13: 978-1-59961-317-8 (v. 2)
ISBN-10: 1-59961-317-4 (v. 2)
ISBN-13: 978-1-59961-318-5 (v. 3)
ISBN-10: 1-59961-318-2 (v. 3)
ISBN-13: 978-1-59961-319-2 (v. 4)
ISBN-10: 1-59961-319-0 (v. 4)
ISBN-13: 978-1-59961-320-8 (v. 5)
ISBN-10: 1-59961-320-4 (v. 5)
ISBN-13: 978-1-59961-321-5 (v. 6)
ISBN-10: 1-59961-321-2 (v. 6)
1. Comic books, strips, etc. I. UDON. II. Title. III. Title: Salvage. IV. Title: Discovery. V. Title: Pet project. VI. Title: Rebuilding. VII. Title: Test mission. VIII. Title: Primary targets.

PN6728.S453 M35 2007
741.5'973--dc22

2006050623

Spotlight

All Spotlight books are reinforced library binding
and manufactured in the United States of America.

Juston Seyfert has just made the discovery of a lifetime: the damaged remains of a 30-foot-tall robot, buried in his father's junkyard! But will his discovery lead to the birth of a new hero...or to unbridled revenge for a life full of hardships...? Stan Lee Presents:

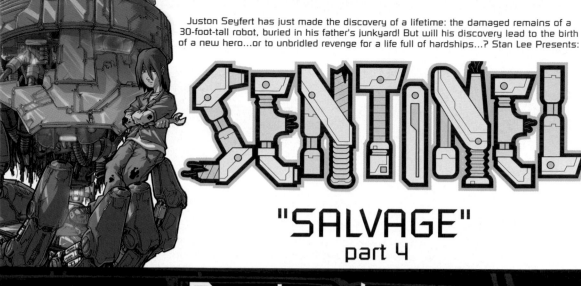

SENTINEL

"SALVAGE"
part 4

Previously...

Juston Seyfert
Our Hero

Pete Seyfert
His Dad

Alex
Best Friend, Part 1

Matt
Best Friend, the Sequel

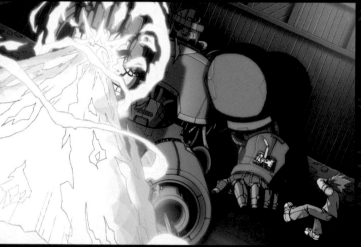

Josh
The Bully

Chris Seyfert
Little Bro

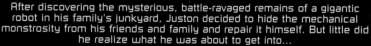

Just when Juston Seyfert thought his life was looking up, everything started crashing down around him again.

After discovering the mysterious, battle-ravaged remains of a gigantic robot in his family's junkyard, Juston decided to hide the mechanical monstrosity from his friends and family and repair it himself. But little did he realize what he was about to get into...

Although the semi-operational robot claimed no memory of its past, Juston's discovery of the machine's high-powered weapons systems prompted him to dig deeper into its origin. And it wasn't long before the truth was uncovered: Juston identified the robot as a Sentinel, a government-built killing machine designed to track down potentially dangerous humans with mutated DNA.

As if the discovery that his pet project is actually a weapon of mass destruction wasn't enough, Juston's personal life continued to fall apart as well. The time spent working on the Sentinel made Juston's closest friends and family feel alienated from him. Senior class bullies continued to plague Juston at every turn. And, worst of all, he learned the hard way that his crush on Jessie, a Senior girl he eats lunch with, was completely one-way.

Overwrought with sadness and frustration, Juston returned to his work on the Sentinel, completely aware of the destruction it could cause...and quite possibly ready to help it do so...

Greg
See "Josh", add Blond

Jessie
The Dream Girl

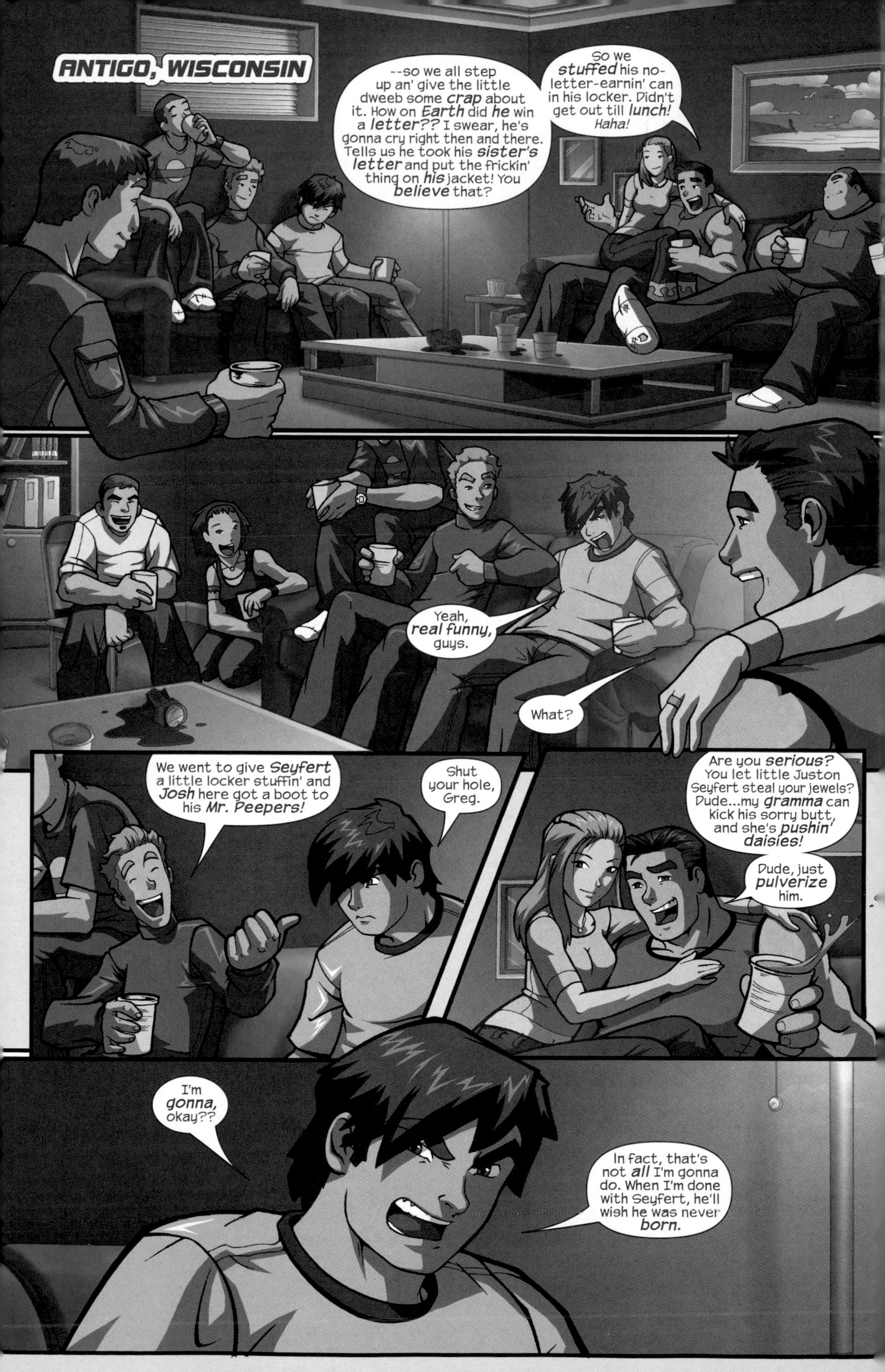
ANTIGO, WISCONSIN
--so we all step up an' give the little dweeb some crap about it. How on Earth did he win a letter?? I swear, he's gonna cry right then and there. Tells us he took his sister's letter and put the frickin' thing on his jacket! You believe that?
So we stuffed his no-letter-earnin' can in his locker. Didn't get out till lunch! Haha!
Yeah, real funny, guys.
What?
We went to give Seyfert a little locker stuffin' and Josh here got a boot to his Mr. Peepers!
Shut your hole, Greg.
Are you serious? You let little Juston Seyfert steal your jewels? Dude...my gramma can kick his sorry butt, and she's pushin' daisies!
Dude, just pulverize him.
I'm gonna, okay??
In fact, that's not all I'm gonna do. When I'm done with Seyfert, he'll wish he was never born.

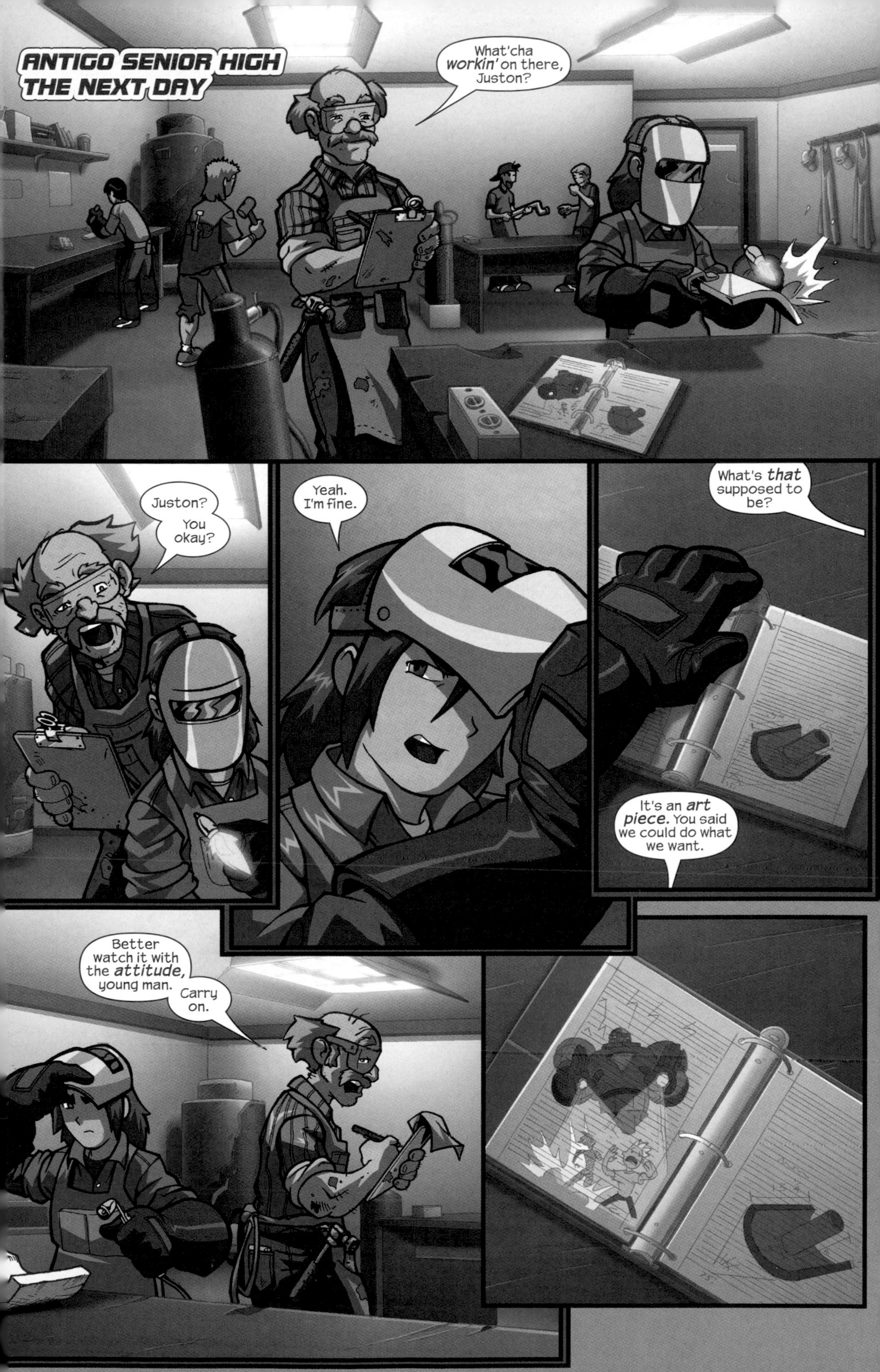
ANTIGO SENIOR HIGH
THE NEXT DAY
What'cha workin' on there, Juston?
Juston?
You okay?
Yeah. I'm fine.
What's that supposed to be?
It's an art piece. You said we could do what we want.
Better watch it with the attitude, young man.
Carry on.

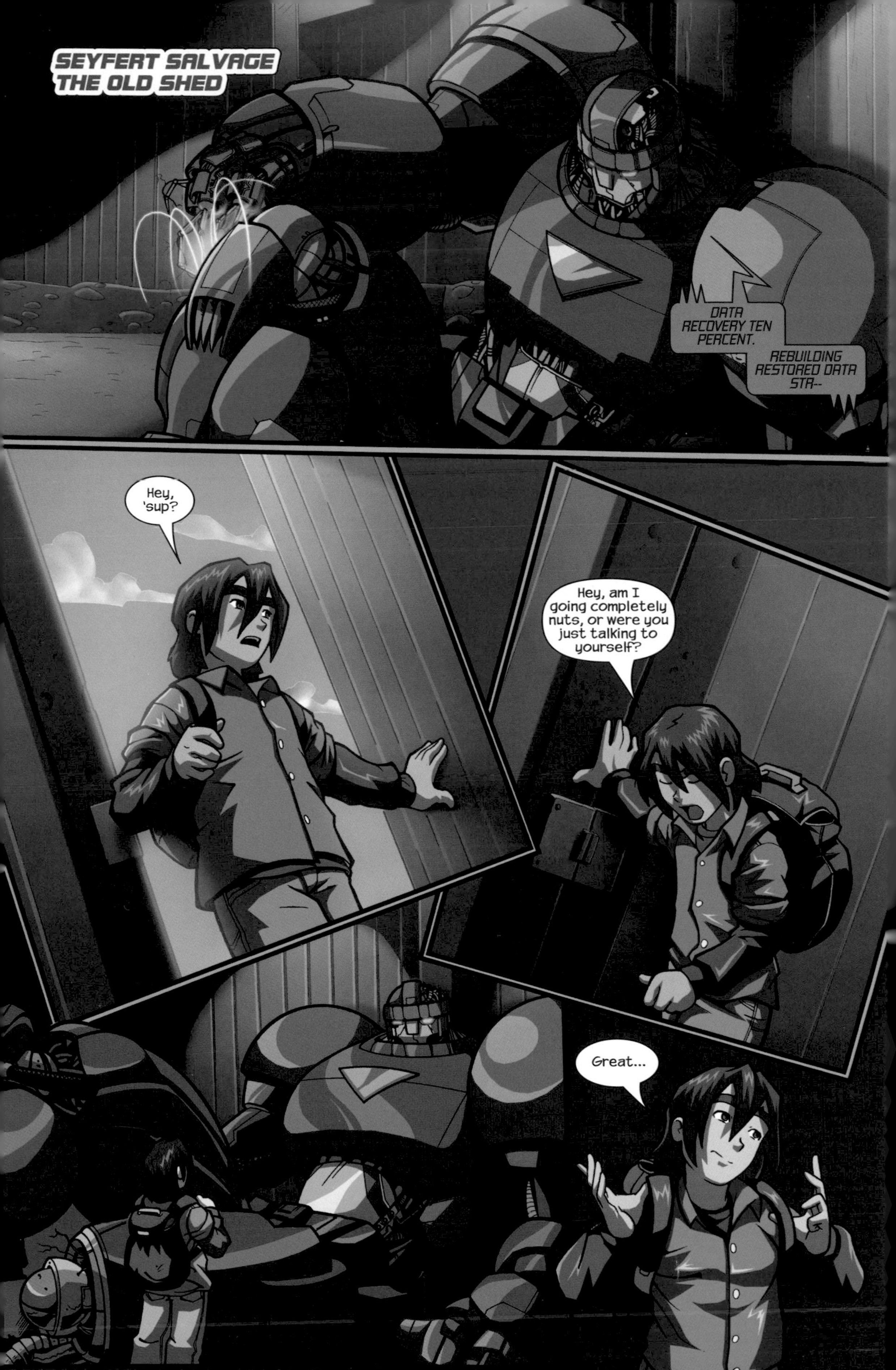
SEYFERT SALVAGE
THE OLD SHED
DATA RECOVERY TEN PERCENT.
REBUILDING RESTORED DATA STR--
Hey, 'sup?
Hey, am I going completely nuts, or were you just talking to yourself?
Great...

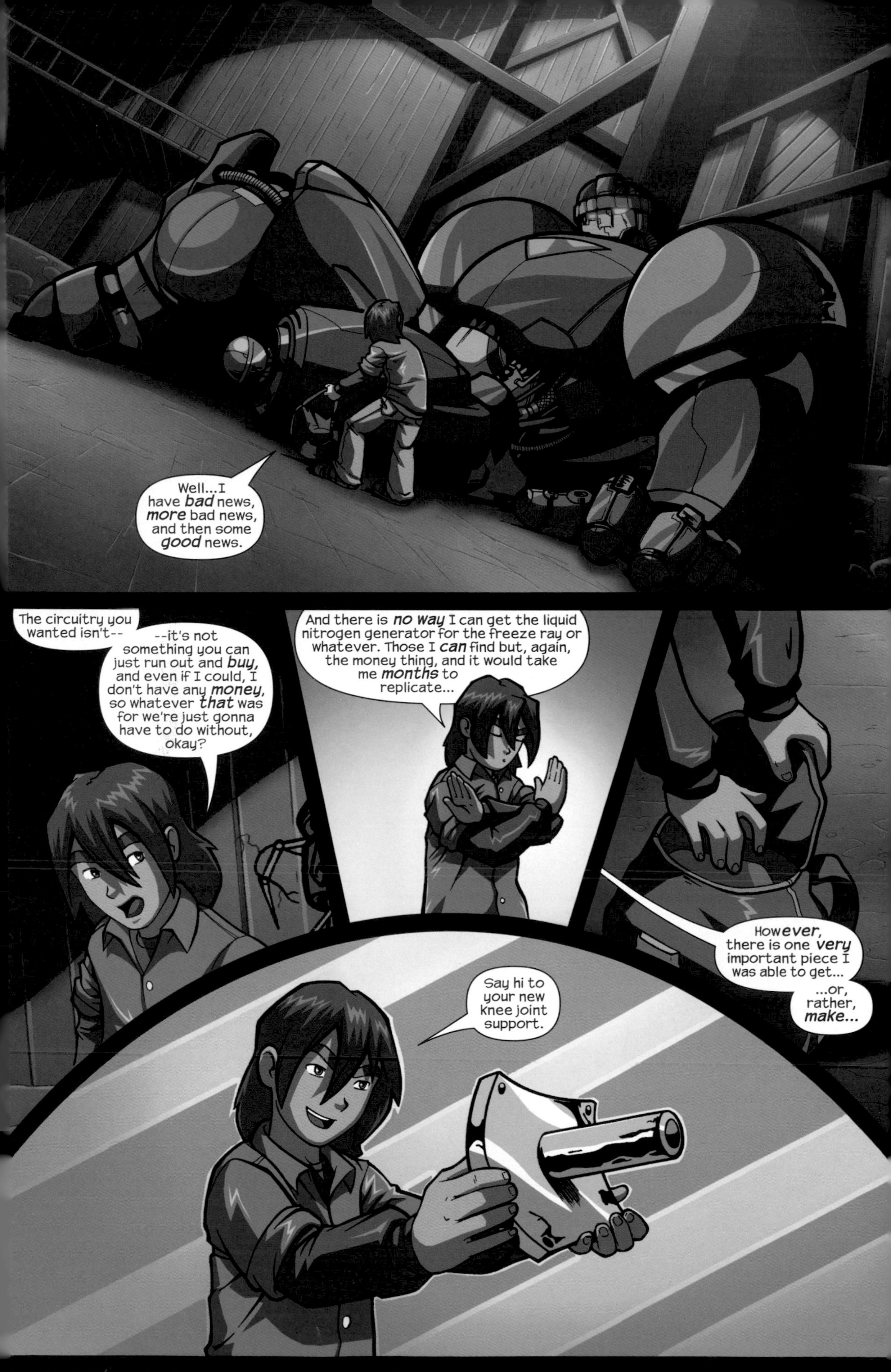
Well...I have *bad* news, *more* bad news, and then some *good* news.
The circuitry you wanted isn't--
--it's not something you can just run out and *buy,* and even if I could, I don't have any *money,* so whatever *that* was for we're just gonna have to do without, okay?
And there is *no way* I can get the liquid nitrogen generator for the freeze ray or whatever. Those I *can* find but, again, the money thing, and it would take me *months* to replicate...
How*ever,* there is one *very* important piece I was able to get...
...or, rather, *make...*
Say hi to your new knee joint support.

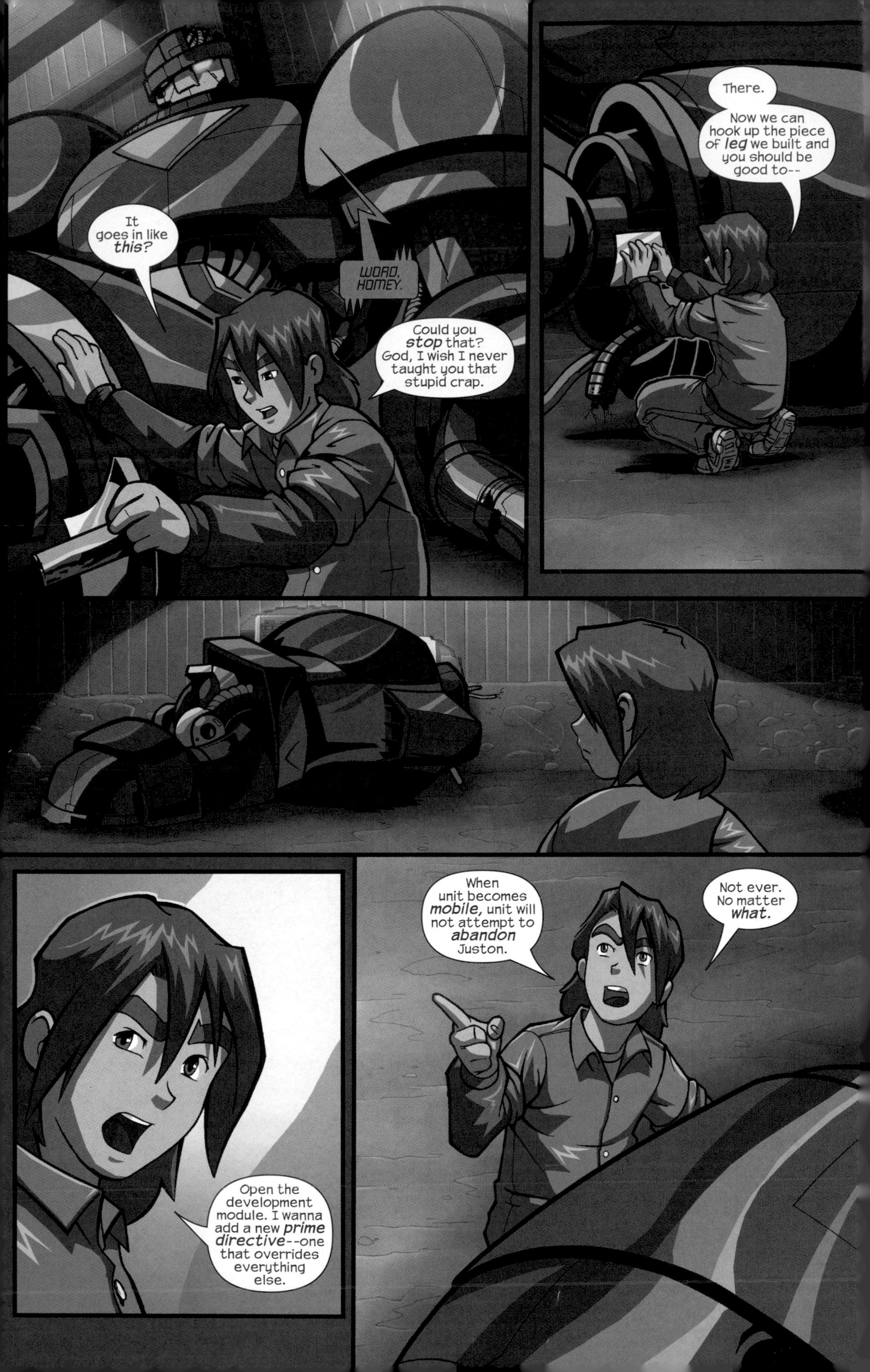
It goes in like *this?*
WORD, HOMEY.
Could you *stop* that? God, I wish I never taught you that stupid crap.
There.
Now we can hook up the piece of *leg* we built and you should be good to--
Open the development module. I wanna add a new *prime directive*--one that overrides everything else.
When unit becomes *mobile,* unit will not attempt to *abandon* Juston.
Not ever. No matter *what.*

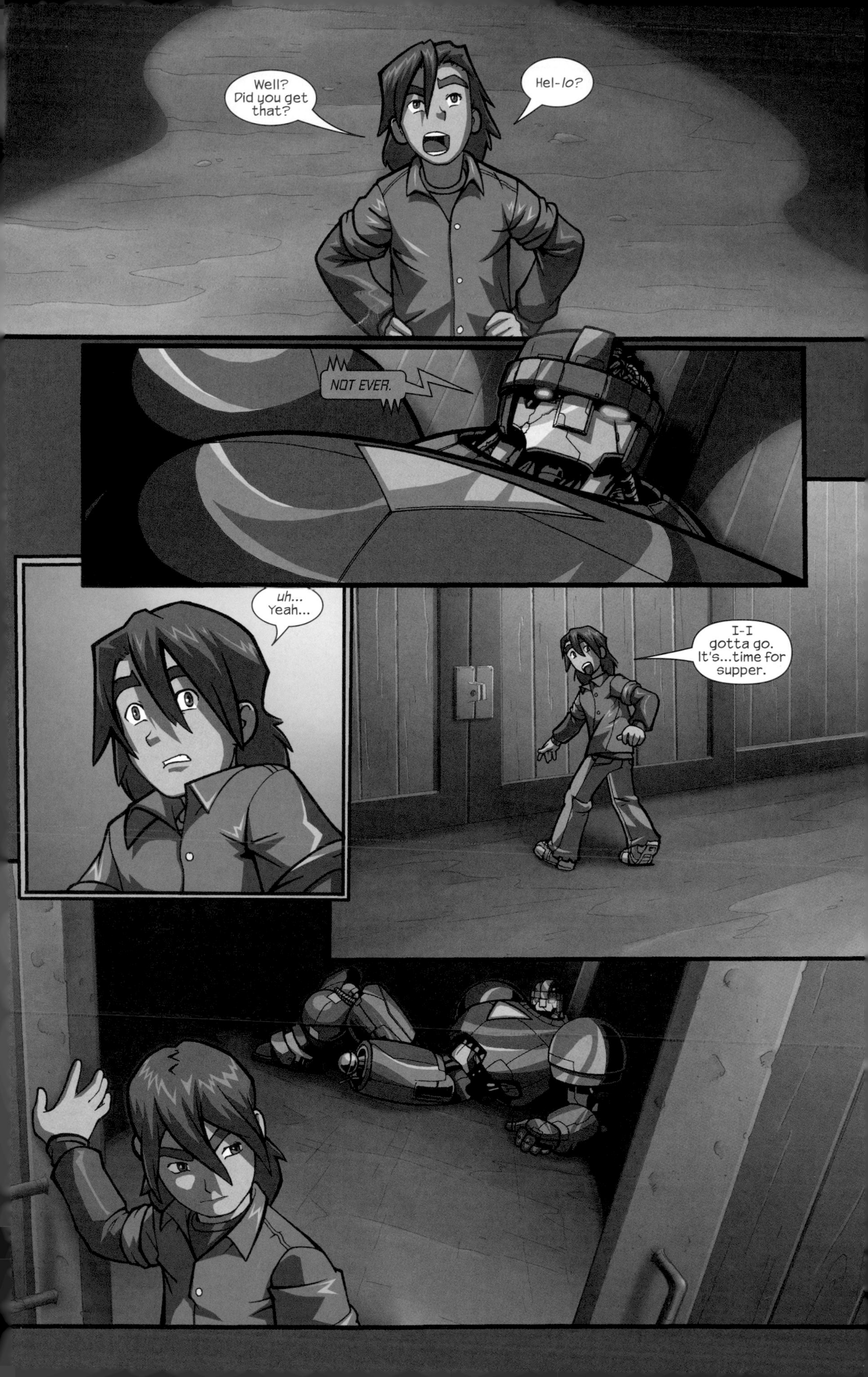
Well? Did you get that?
Hel-lo?
NOT EVER.
uh... Yeah...
I-I gotta go. It's...time for supper.

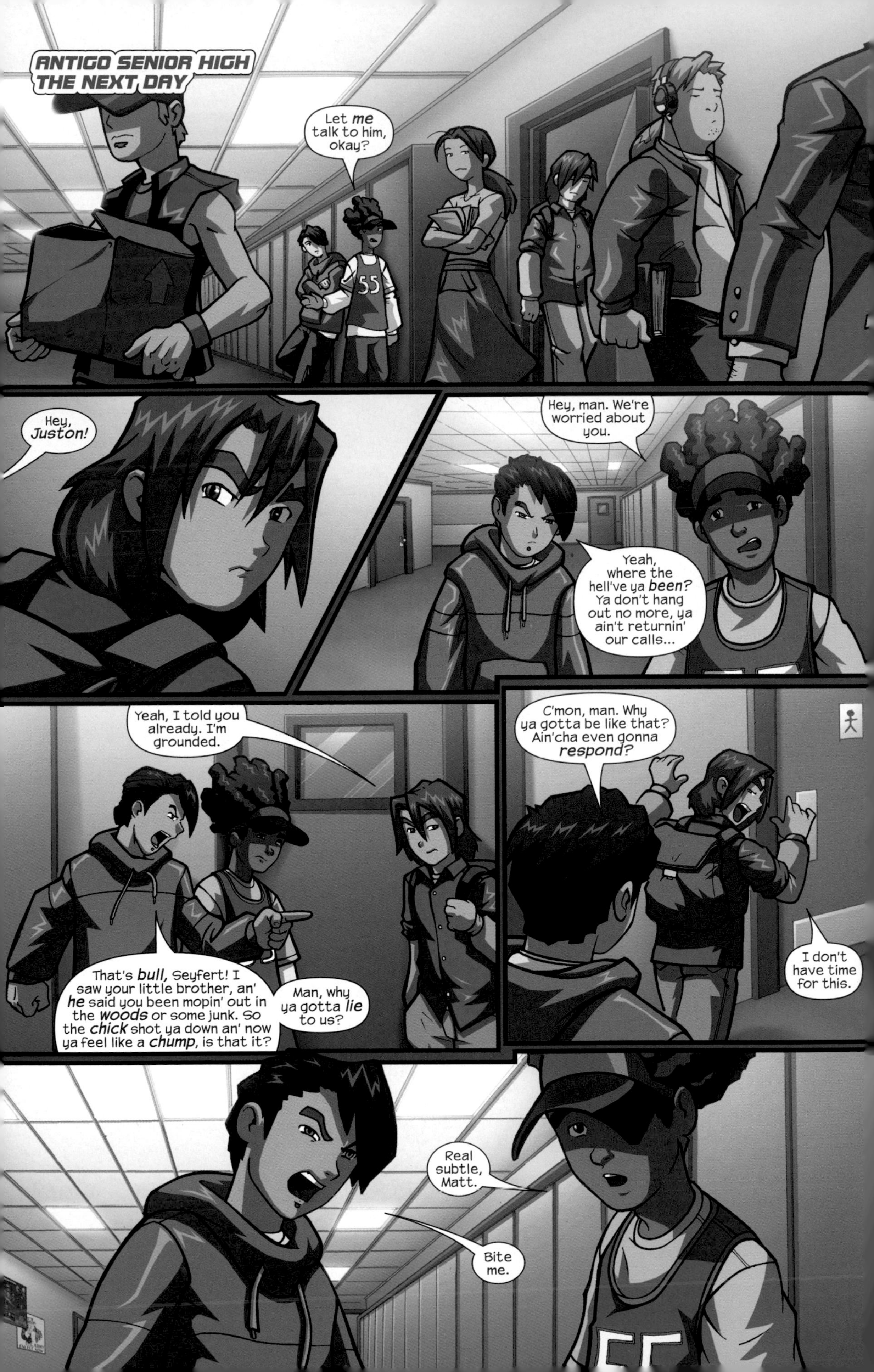
ANTIGO SENIOR HIGH
THE NEXT DAY
Let me talk to him, okay?
Hey, Juston!
Hey, man. We're worried about you.
Yeah, where the hell've ya been? Ya don't hang out no more, ya ain't returnin' our calls...
Yeah, I told you already. I'm grounded.
That's bull, Seyfert! I saw your little brother, an' he said you been mopin' out in the woods or some junk. So the chick shot ya down an' now ya feel like a chump, is that it?
Man, why ya gotta lie to us?
C'mon, man. Why ya gotta be like that? Ain'cha even gonna respond?
I don't have time for this.
Real subtle, Matt.
Bite me.

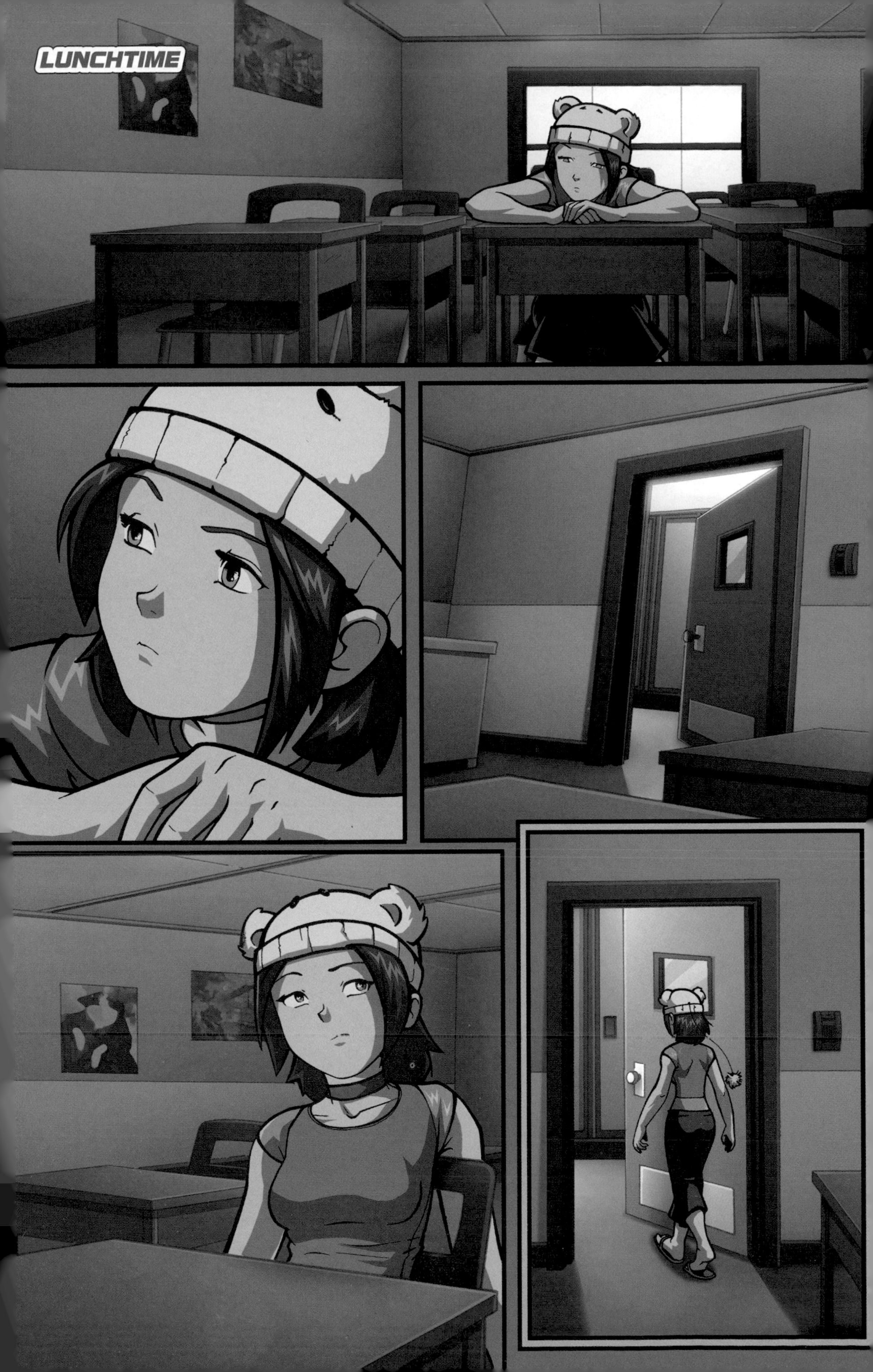
LUNCHTIME

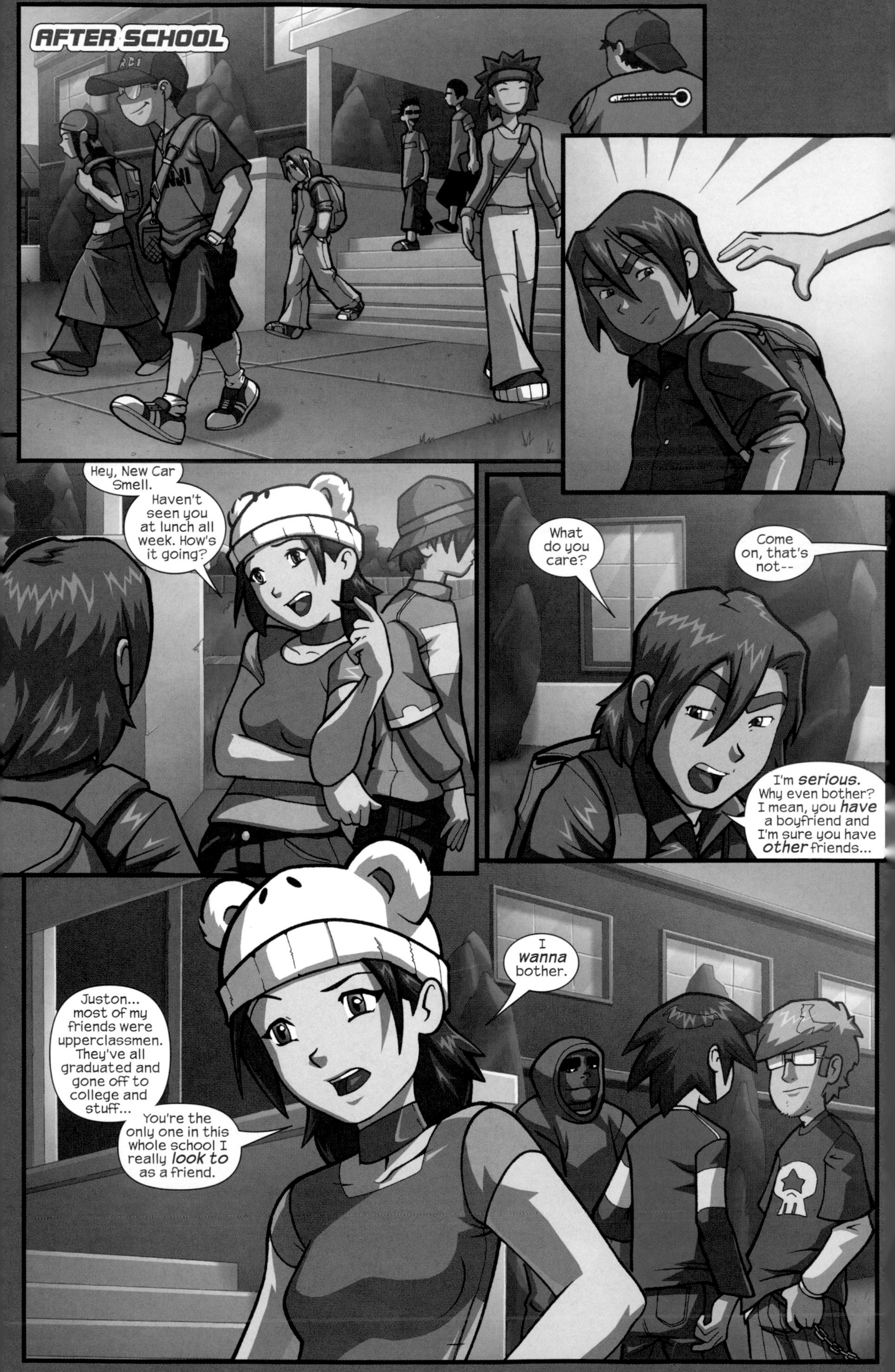
AFTER SCHOOL
Hey, New Car Smell. Haven't seen you at lunch all week. How's it going?
What do you care?
Come on, that's not--
I'm serious. Why even bother? I mean, you have a boyfriend and I'm sure you have other friends...
I wanna bother.
Juston... most of my friends were upperclassmen. They've all graduated and gone off to college and stuff...
You're the only one in this whole school I really look to as a friend.

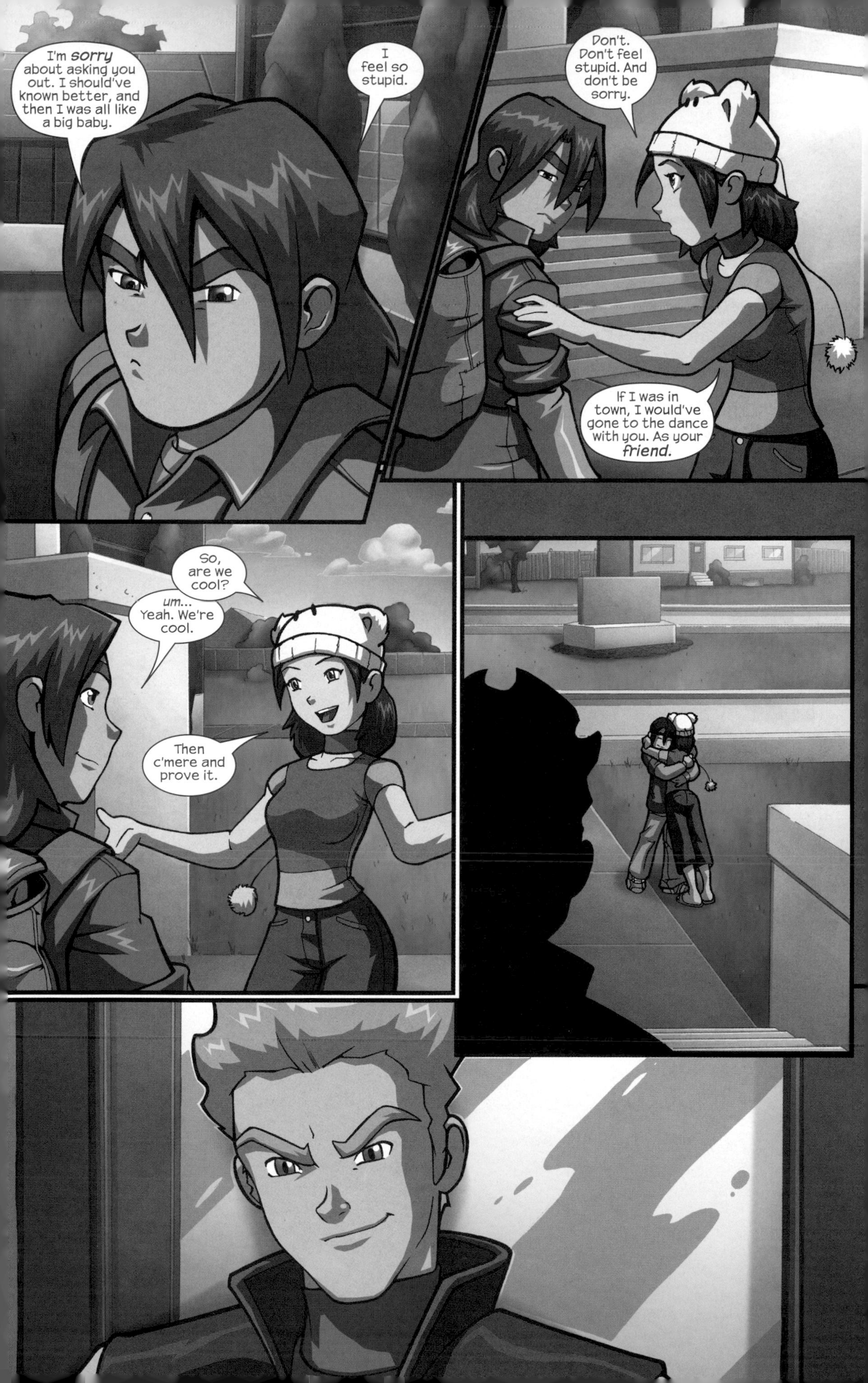
I'm sorry about asking you out. I should've known better, and then I was all like a big baby.
I feel so stupid.
Don't. Don't feel stupid. And don't be sorry.
If I was in town, I would've gone to the dance with you. As your friend.
So, are we cool?
um... Yeah. We're cool.
Then c'mere and prove it.

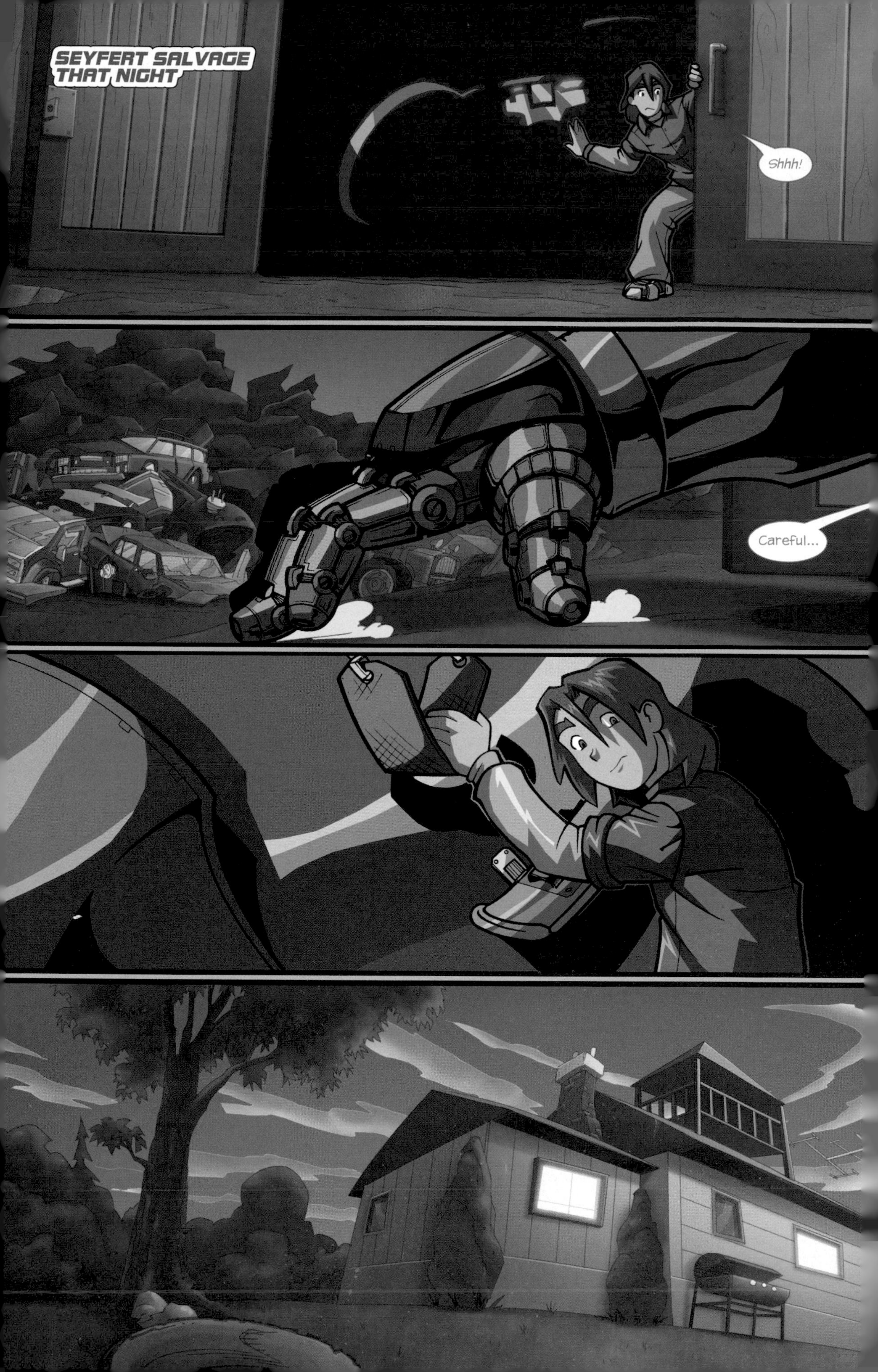
SEYFERT SALVAGE
THAT NIGHT
Shhh!
Careful...

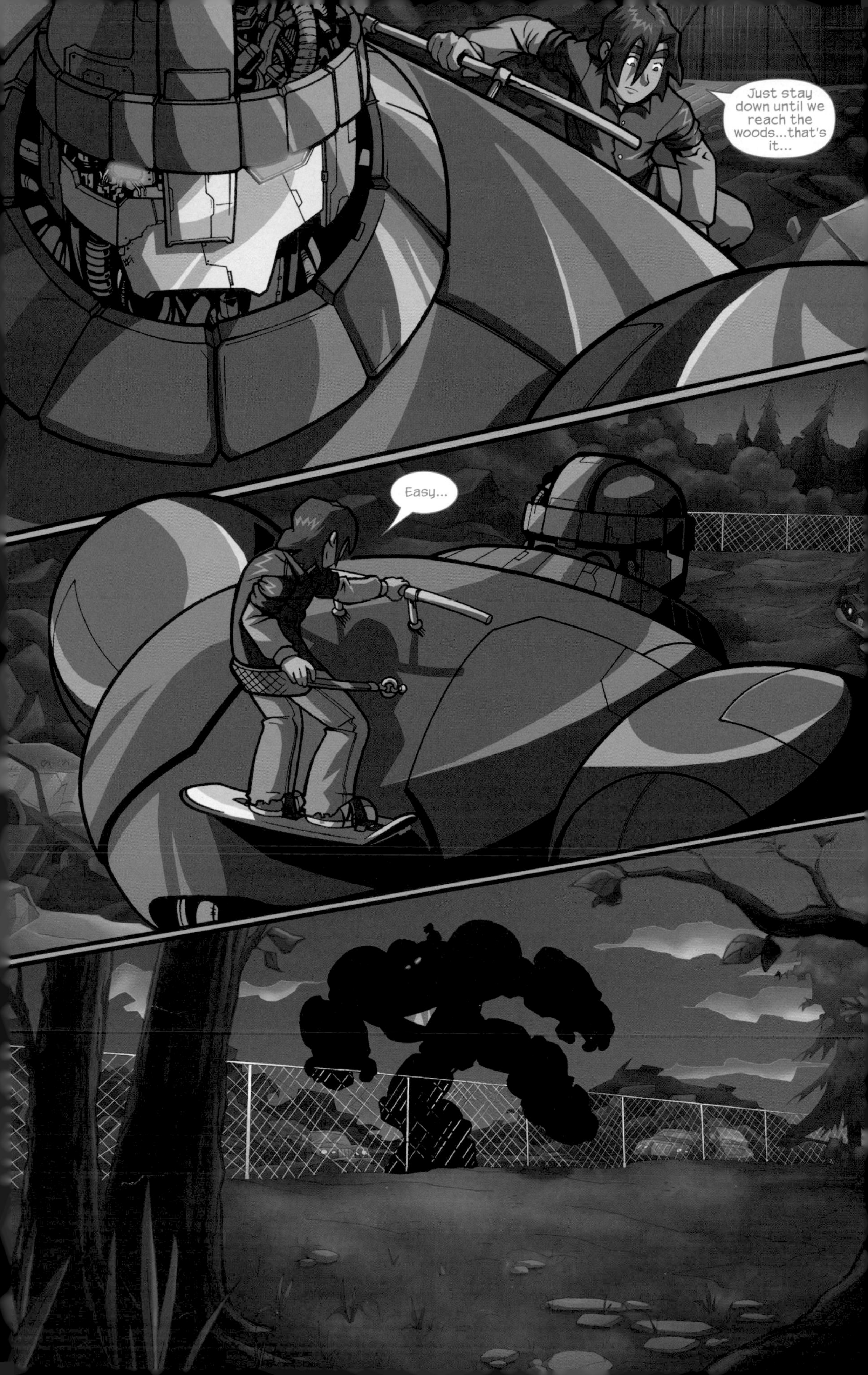
Just stay down until we reach the woods...that's it...
Easy...

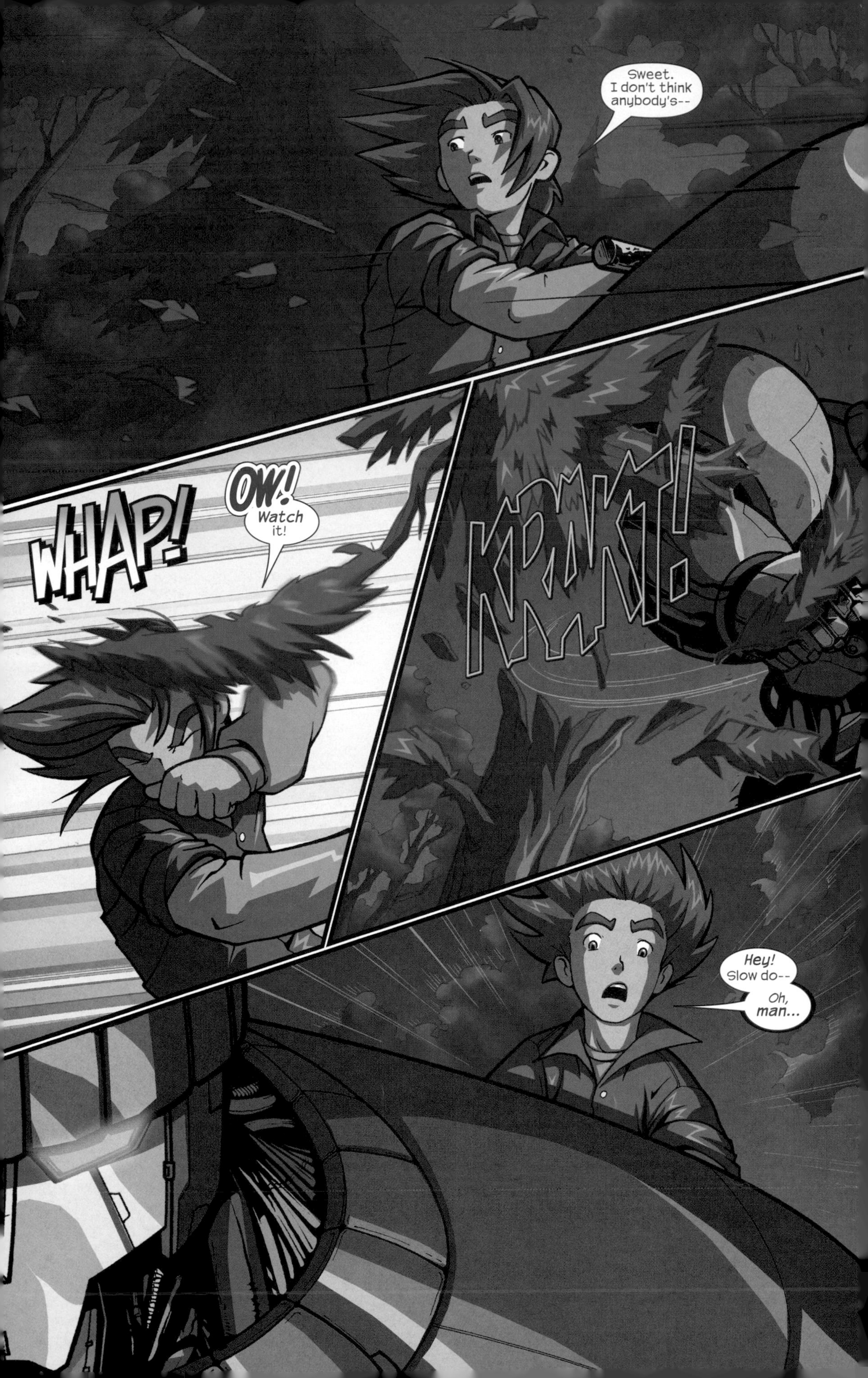
Sweet. I don't think anybody's--
WHAP!
OW! Watch it!
KRAKT!
Hey! Slow do--
Oh, man...

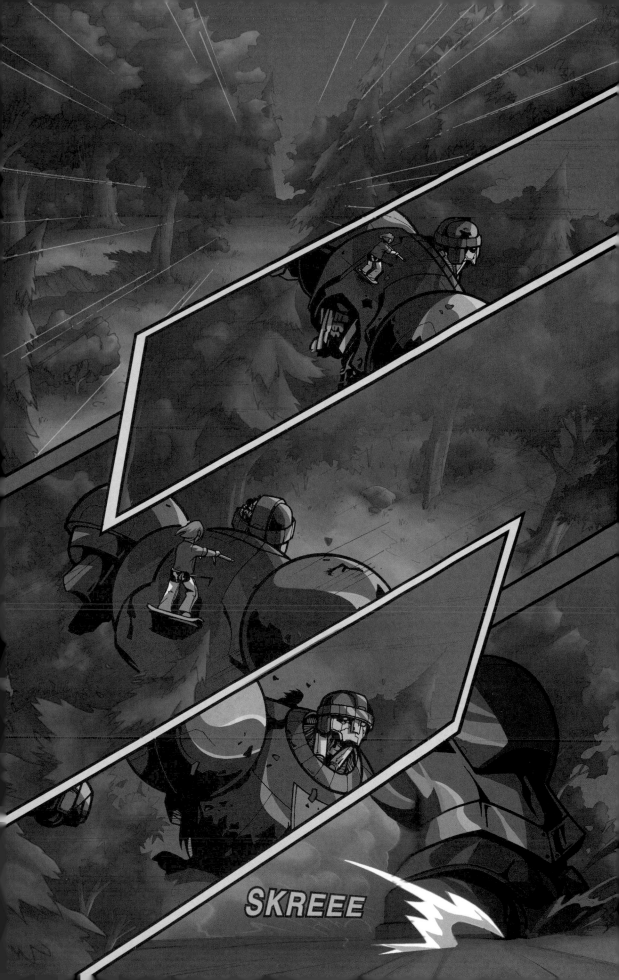

SKREEE

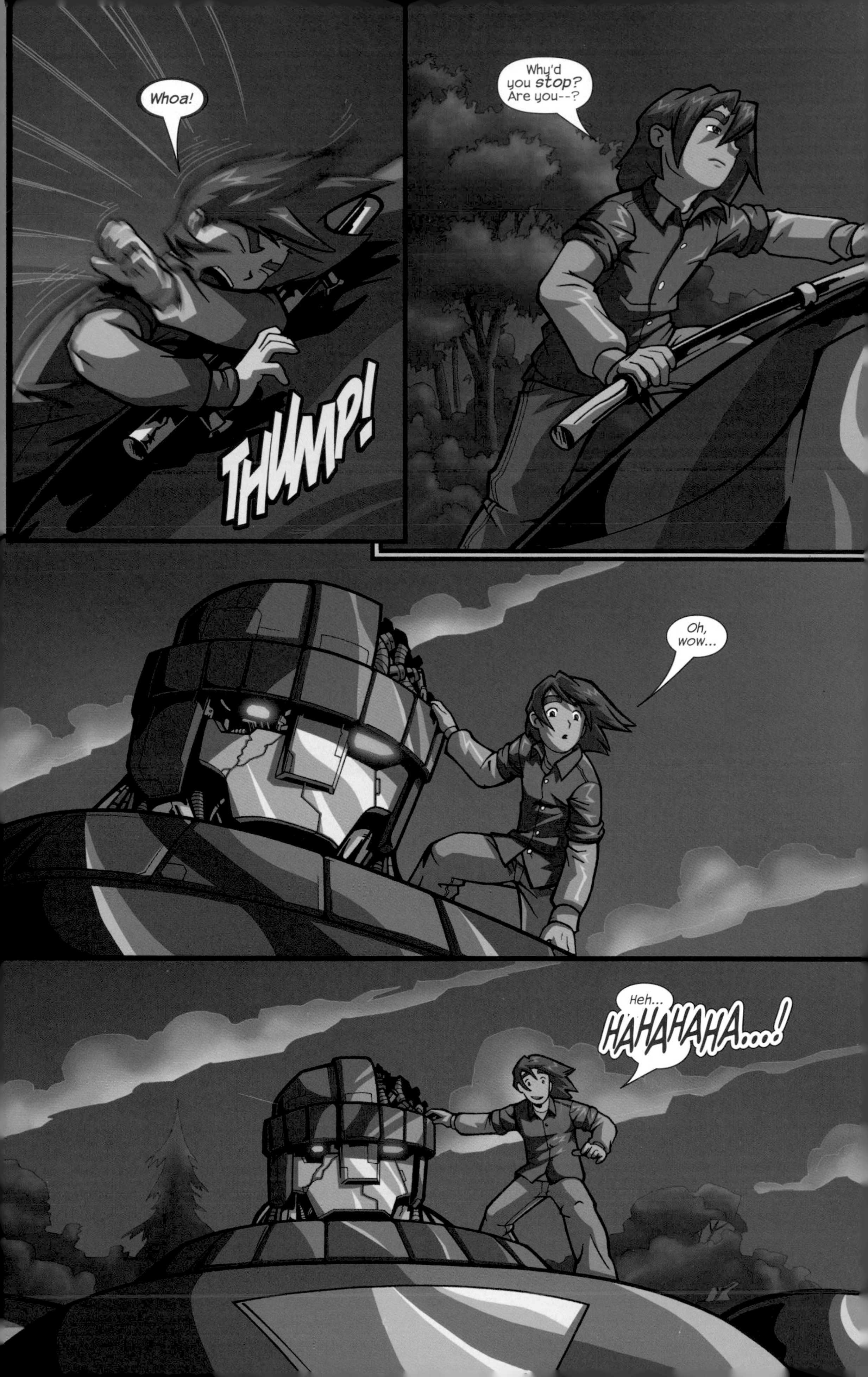
Whoa!
THUMP!
Why'd you stop? Are you--?
Oh, wow...
Heh...
HAHAHAHA...!

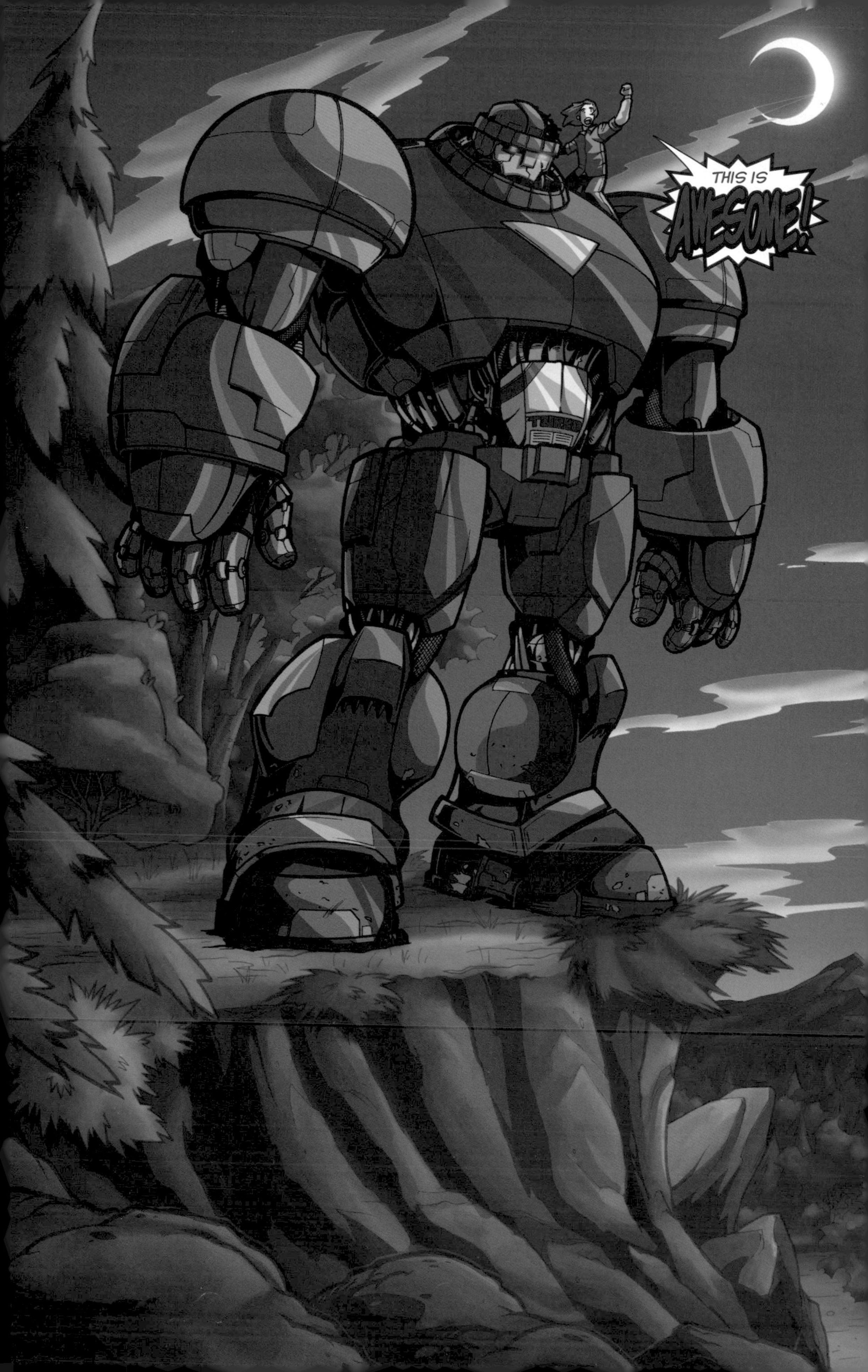
THIS IS AWESOME!

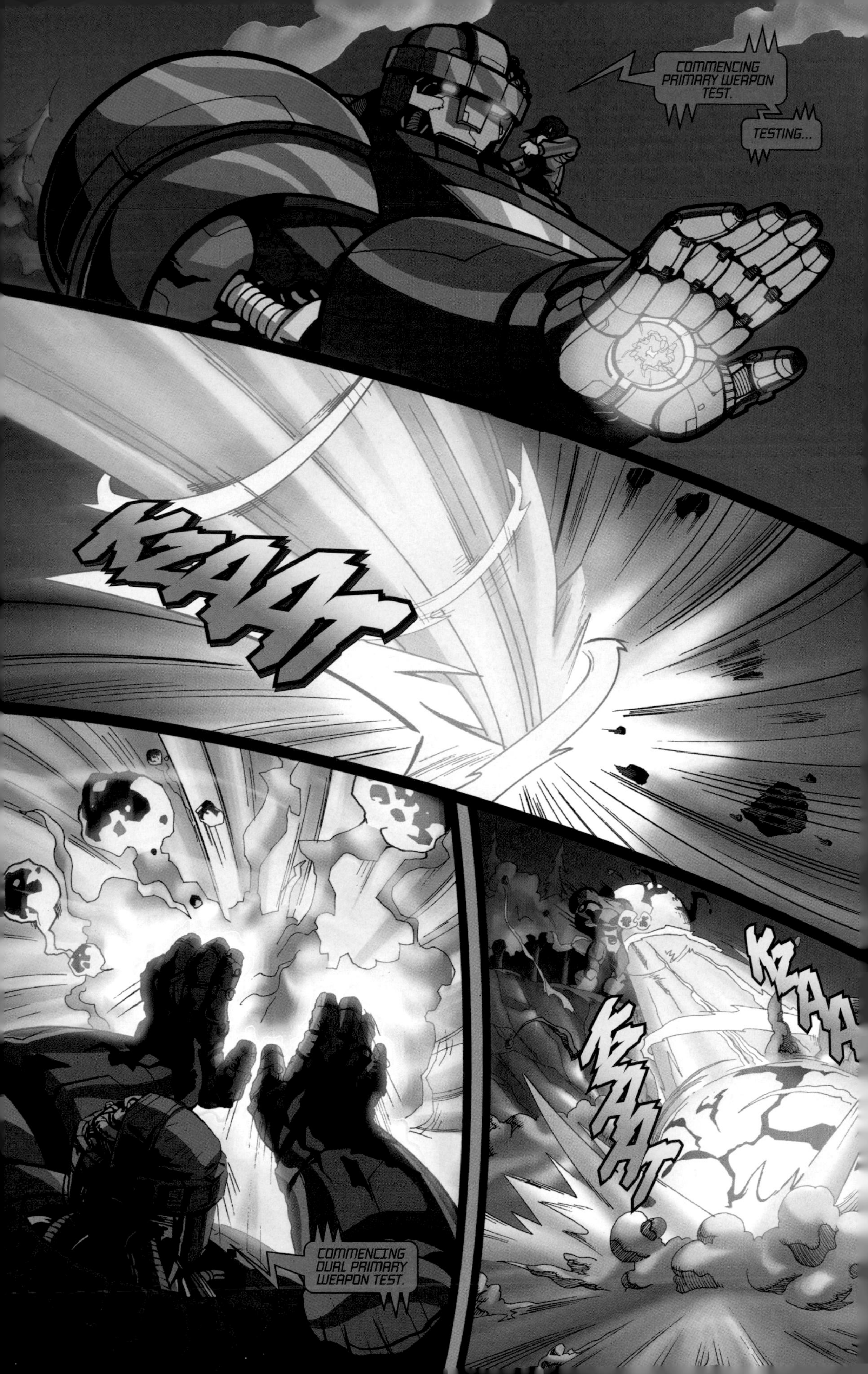

COMMENCING PRIMARY WEAPON TEST.
TESTING...
KZAAT
COMMENCING DUAL PRIMARY WEAPON TEST.
KZAAT
KZAAA

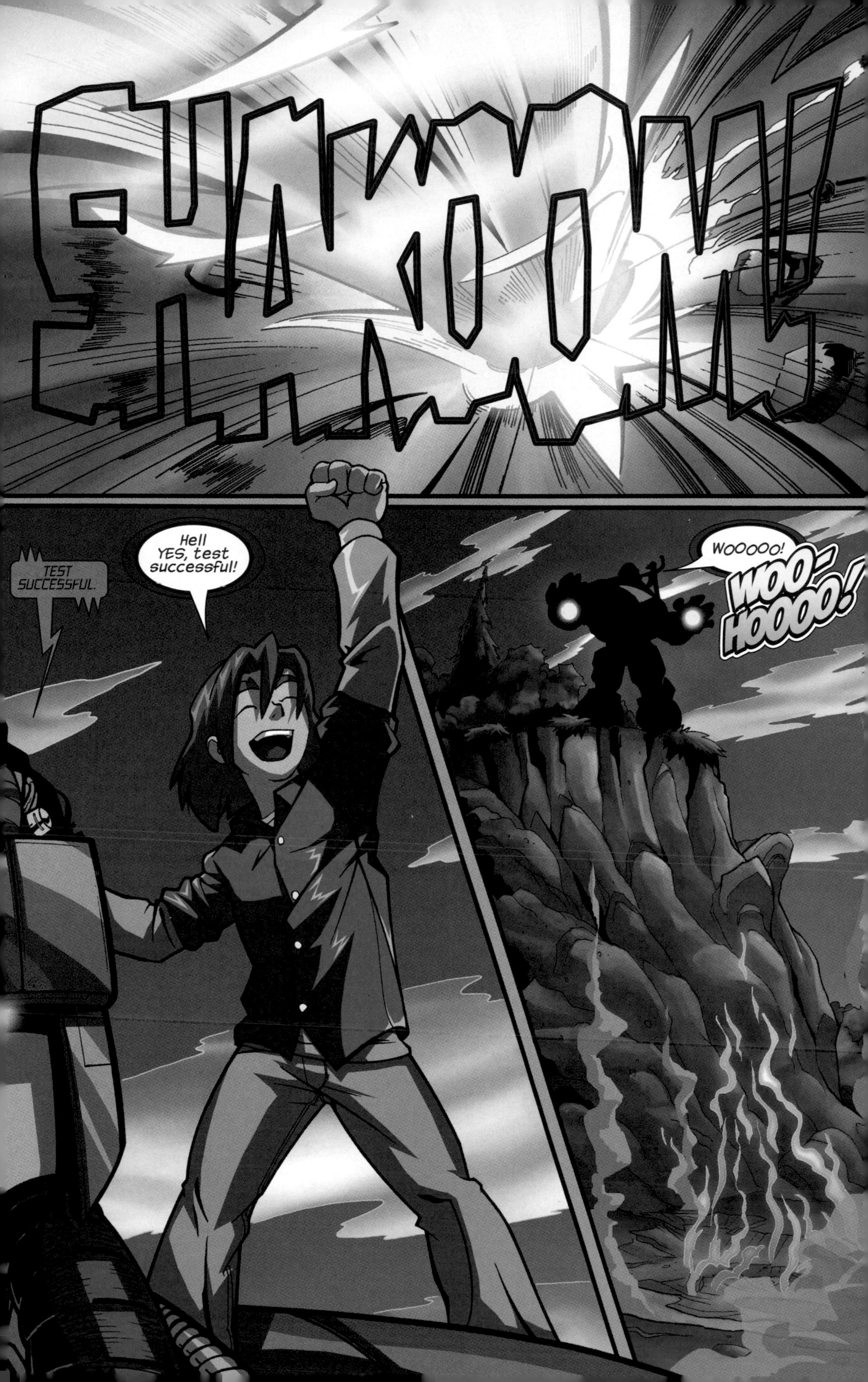
SHAKOOM!
TEST SUCCESSFUL.
Hell YES, test successful!
WOOOOO!
WOO-HOOOO!

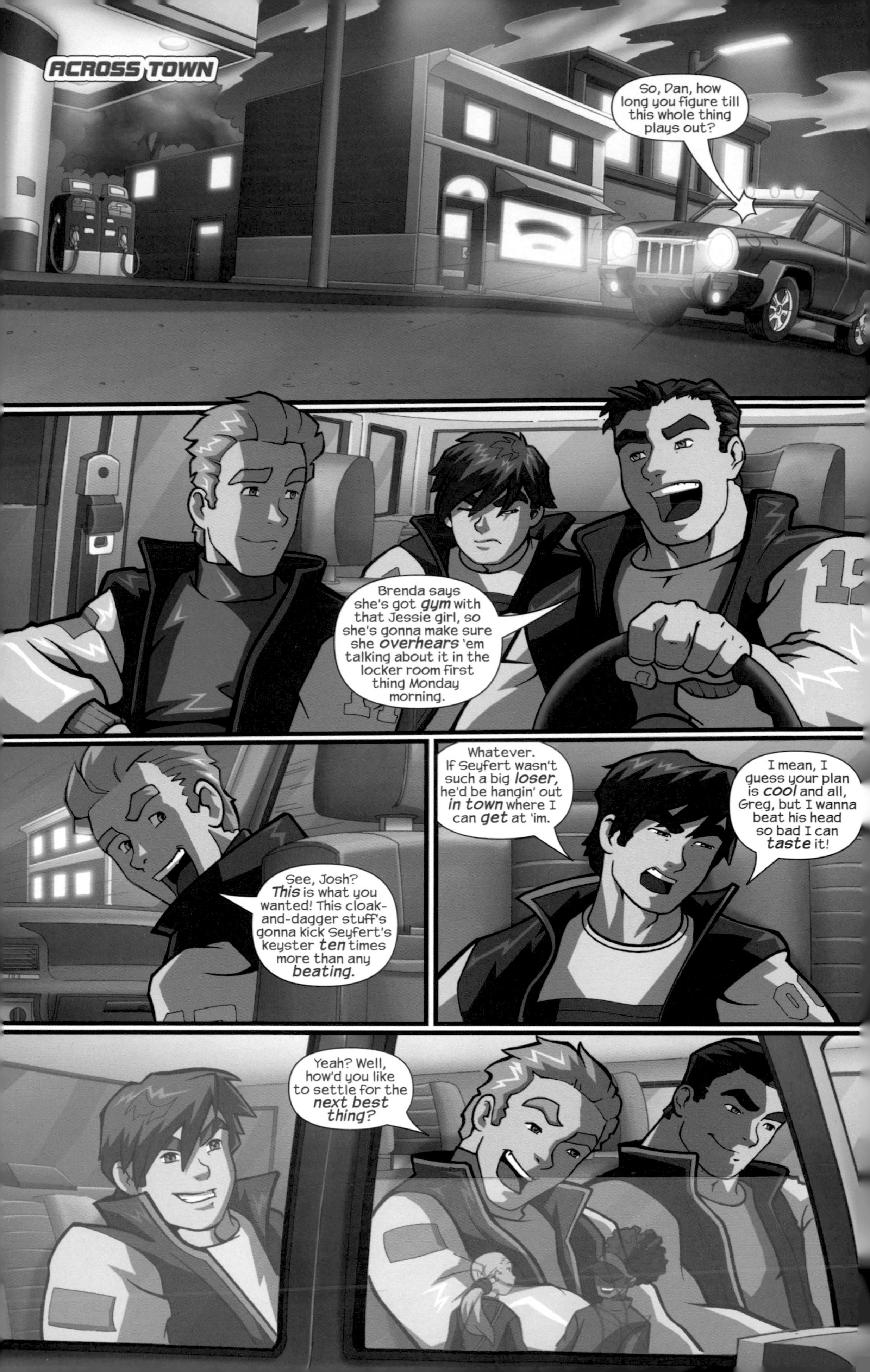
ACROSS TOWN
So, Dan, how long you figure till this whole thing plays out?
Brenda says she's got gym with that Jessie girl, so she's gonna make sure she overhears 'em talking about it in the locker room first thing Monday morning.
See, Josh? This is what you wanted! This cloak-and-dagger stuff's gonna kick Seyfert's keyster ten times more than any beating.
Whatever. If Seyfert wasn't such a big loser, he'd be hangin' out in town where I can get at 'im.
I mean, I guess your plan is cool and all, Greg, but I wanna beat his head so bad I can taste it!
Yeah? Well, how'd you like to settle for the next best thing?

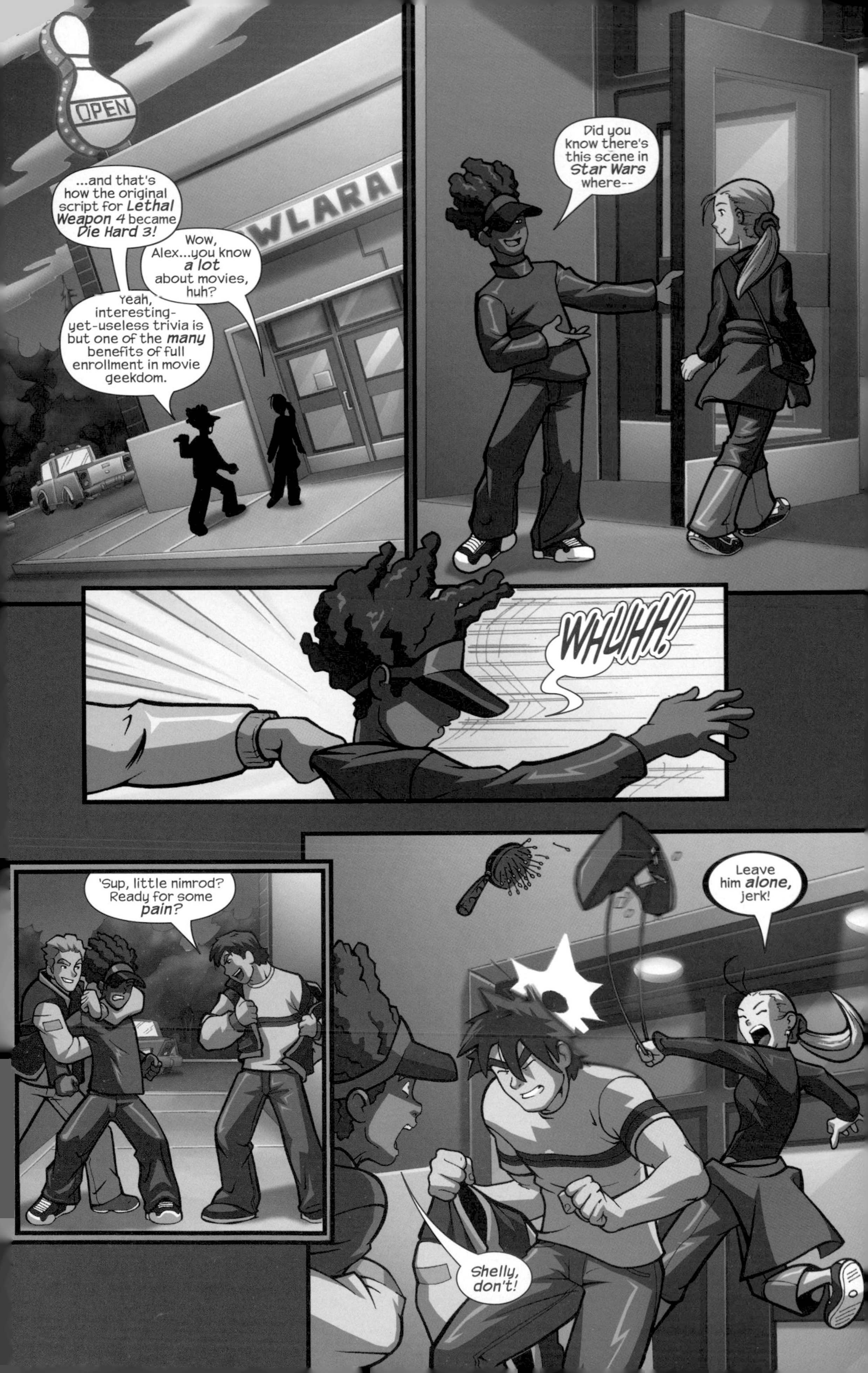
OPEN
WLARA
...and that's how the original script for Lethal Weapon 4 became Die Hard 3!
Wow, Alex...you know a lot about movies, huh?
Yeah, interesting-yet-useless trivia is but one of the many benefits of full enrollment in movie geekdom.
Did you know there's this scene in Star Wars where--
WHUHH!
'Sup, little nimrod? Ready for some pain?
Leave him alone, jerk!
Shelly, don't!

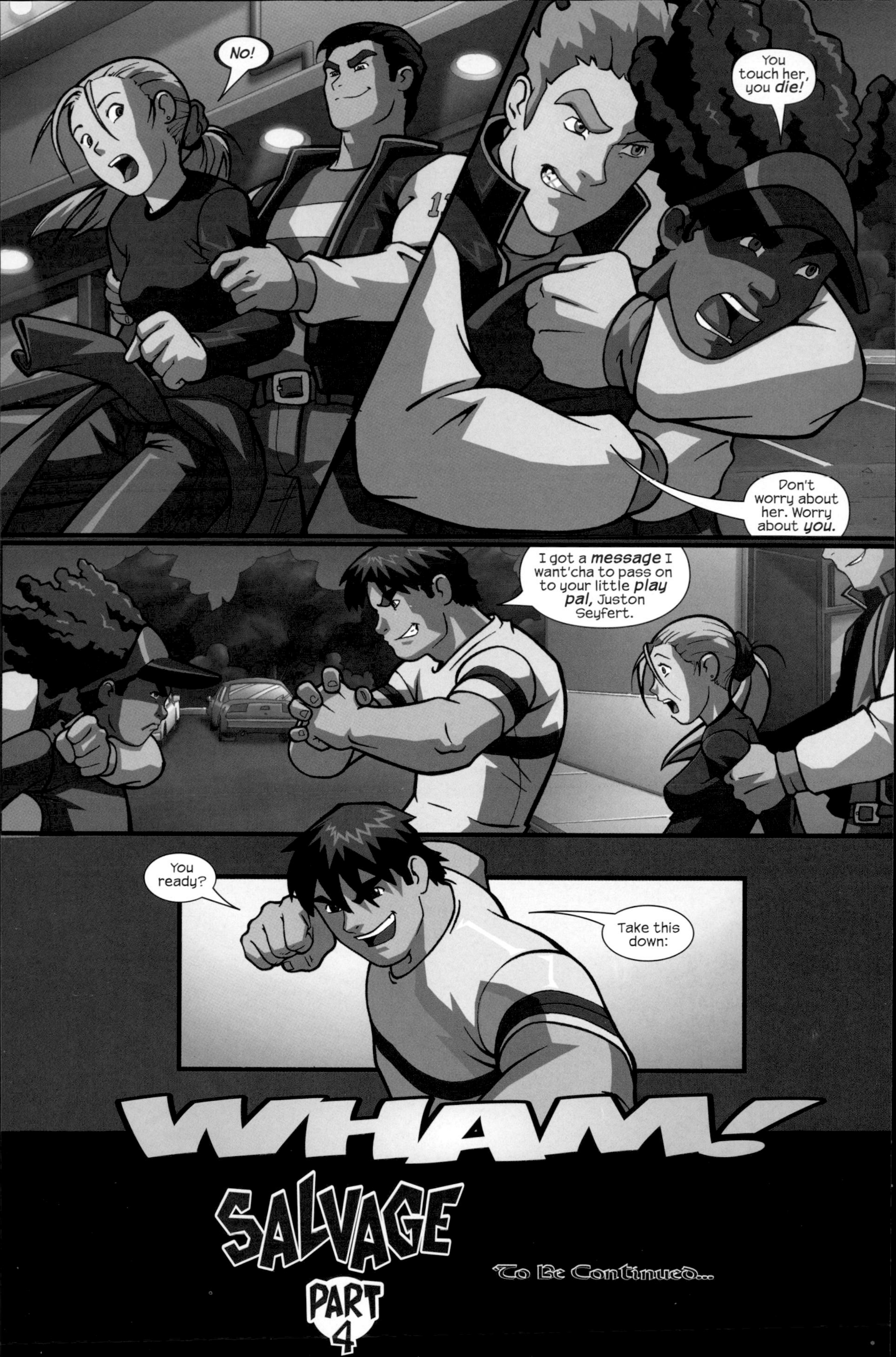
No!
You touch her, you *die!*
Don't worry about her. Worry about *you.*
I got a *message* I want'cha to pass on to your little *play pal,* Juston Seyfert.
You ready?
Take this down:
WHAM!
SALVAGE PART 4
To Be Continued...